Luna
the Loom Band
Fairy

by Daisy Meadows

ORCHARD

www.rainbowmagic.co.uk

The Fairyland Palace

Seeing Pool

Café

Kirsty's House

Wetherbury Village

Luna

the Loom Band

Fairy

To Amelie, from the fairies

Special thanks to
Rachel Elliot

ORCHARD BOOKS
338 Euston Road, London NW1 3BH
Orchard Books Australia
Level 17/207 Kent Street, Sydney, NSW 2000
A Paperback Original

First published in 2014 by Orchard Books

A CIP catalogue record for this book is available
from the British Library.

ISBN 978 1 40833 898 8
1 3 5 7 9 10 8 6 4 2

Printed in Great Britain

The paper and board used in this paperback are natural recyclable
products made from wood grown in sustainable forests. The
manufacturing processes conform to the environmental regulations
of the country of origin.

Orchard Books is a division of Hachette Children's Books,
an Hachette UK company

www.hachette.co.uk

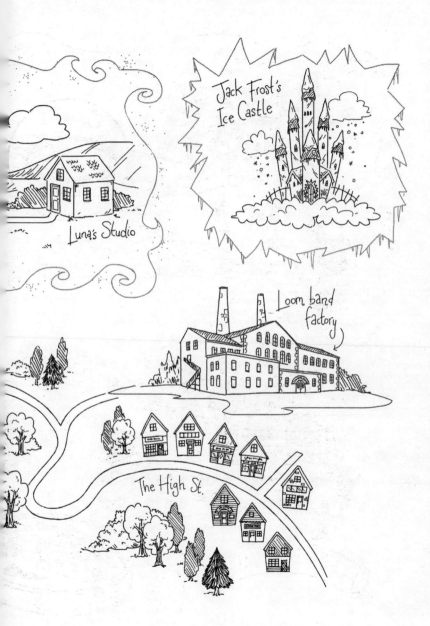

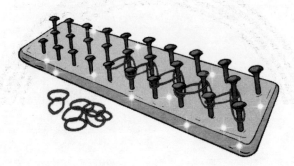

Jack Frost's Spell

Loom-band art is all the rage.
It's fun no matter what your age.
They say beginners must start small,
But that's no kind of fun at all!

I'm thinking big! I will not wait.
Luna's loom will make me great.
Let humans' loom bands twang and snap.
I'll weave while they get in a flap!

Contents

Workshop Shock

The sound of a car engine grew louder, and Kirsty Tate jumped up from the sitting-room table for the fifth time that morning. She was expecting her best friend, Rachel Walker, who was coming to stay for the weekend. But the car went past the house without stopping.

Kirsty returned to the table, where she was making a rainbow-coloured loom-band bracelet.

"That looks good," said Mrs Tate, peering over her daughter's shoulder. "Is it for Rachel?"

Kirsty nodded. "It's a special friendship bracelet in our favourite colours," she explained.

Mrs Tate smiled, but Kirsty knew that her mother didn't really understand. Rachel and Kirsty loved rainbows for a secret, very special reason – because they reminded them of the Rainbow Fairies. Kirsty and Rachel were friends with the fairies, and the Rainbow Fairies were the first ones they had ever met.

Just as Kirsty finished the bracelet and took it off the loom, she heard a car stop

on the road outside. She dashed to the
window, and there was Rachel hopping
out of her parents' car.

"She's here!" called Kirsty.

Without even stopping to change out
of her slippers, she ran out to meet her
best friend and they shared a happy hug.

"I've made
something for
you," said
Kirsty, pressing
the bracelet
into Rachel's
hand. "I hope
you like it."

"I love it,"
said Rachel,
laughing as she pulled
the bracelet onto her wrist.

"But guess what I made for you too!"

She pulled an identical rainbow-coloured loom-band bracelet out of her pocket!

"It's perfect," said Kirsty, joining in with Rachel's laughter and putting on the bracelet.

Mrs Tate was waiting to greet the Walkers in the doorway.

"Hello, Rachel," she said. "I see that you love loom bands too!"

"They're brilliant," said Rachel with a smile.

"There's a loom-band workshop this morning in the café at the end of our road," said Mrs Tate. "Perhaps you would like to go?"

Rachel and Kirsty let out squeals of excitement.

"Really?"

"Oh, please can we?"

Mr and Mrs Walker agreed, and Mrs Tate nodded.

"You'd better hurry, though," she said, looking at her watch. "It starts in five minutes!"

When the girls arrived at the café, the first thing they saw was a very unusual bicycle leaning against the window outside. The seat cover was made of red and white loom bands, and there were loom bands in every possible colour twisted all around the spokes.

"Wow, that's amazing," said Kirsty. "I wish I could do that!"

"Maybe we'll learn how today!" said Rachel, pushing open the door of the café. "Come on!"

The café was buzzing with noise and colour. Boys and girls of all different ages were crowded around tables laden with loom bands, looms, hooks and patterns. Everyone was chattering and

comparing their projects.

Rachel and Kirsty made their way through the obstacle course of tables and chairs, and found some spare seats next to a boy in a red-and-white T-shirt.

"Hello," said the boy. "I'm Oscar."

"I'm Rachel and this is Kirsty," said Rachel with a smile. "Isn't this exciting? What are you hoping to learn?"

"I want to make some handlebar covers for my bike," said Oscar.

"Oh, is that your amazing bike outside?" Kirsty asked.

Oscar went red with pride, but before he could speak again a tall, blonde lady stood up and clapped her hands.

"Hi, everyone," she said. "I'm Sarah, and I'm going to help you out with some new loom-band projects today.

I can't wait to get started! First, please decide what you are going to make and choose a loom and some bands. I will walk around and have a chat with each of you."

The buzz of chatter soon began again as everyone tried to decide what to make. Rachel chose a watch strap and Kirsty planned a butterfly hairclip. As they pulled their looms towards them, they heard a loud, grumpy voice.

"These patterns are all stupid! Get me some different ones NOW!"

"I recognise that voice," said Rachel with a frown.

"Me too," said Kirsty, peering across the crowded café to see who was speaking.

It was a teenage boy with his back to

them. He was wearing a baggy football shirt, jeans and a bright blue cap pulled low over his hair.

"These loom bands don't work properly," he shouted at Sarah.

At that moment he half turned towards the girls, and they saw at once that it was Jack Frost in disguise!

Mission to Fairyland

"You just need to be patient and keep trying," Sarah said. "You'll get the hang of it."

"I don't want to make a stupid bracelet," said Jack Frost in a peevish voice. "I want to make a long, flowing coat."

"Just start with something small," said Sarah, placing a pattern in front of him. "A coat would take a very long time for a beginner."

She moved away to the next table, and Jack Frost scowled after her. Then he jumped down from his seat and headed towards the door.

"Someone as important as *me* shouldn't have to be patient or start small," the girls heard him snap as he stomped past them. "I know how to make my coat instantly – with a little help from those annoying fairies!"

"He's going to cause trouble in Fairyland," said Rachel. "We have to warn the fairies!"

The girls followed Jack Frost out of the café and saw him turn the corner at

the end of the street.
They ran after
him, but when
they reached
the corner he
was nowhere
to be seen.

"He must
have gone to
Fairyland already,"
said Rachel.

Kirsty pulled out the locket that she
always wore from under her T-shirt, and
Rachel did the same, looking around to
check that no one was watching. Their
lockets were filled with fairy dust that
could carry them to Fairyland. Together,
the girls sprinkled the fairy dust over
themselves.

Instantly the street around them shimmered as they shrank to fairy size and gauzy wings appeared on their backs. They felt themselves whirling into the air and sparkles surrounded them as they left the human world. Seconds later they were standing in the gardens of the Fairyland Palace.

"Rachel! Kirsty!" called a friendly voice in surprise.

The girls turned and saw Queen
Titania coming towards them with her
hands held out in welcome. Rachel
and Kirsty both curtseyed, and quickly
explained what had happened.

"I see," said the queen, looking serious.
"Thank you for coming to warn us. First
of all, let me refill your lockets."

A wave of her wand replaced the
fairy dust in the girls' lockets, and they
thanked her and tucked them back under
their T-shirts.

"Come with me to the Seeing Pool,"
said the queen. "Perhaps we can find out
if Jack Frost is up to any mischief."

The girls followed Queen Titania
through the beautiful palace gardens to
the golden Seeing Pool. The magical
waters shimmered in the sunlight, but
when the queen waved her wand over
the pool, a moving picture began to
form. They could see Jack Frost creeping
along beside a coral-pink wall. His
shoulders were hunched and his head was
bowed low. There was a single goblin
behind him, also looking very sneaky. As
they watched, the goblin coughed and

Jack Frost turned around with his finger to his lips.

"Shh!" he said. "This is my chance. I'm going to have my dream loom-band coat – no matter what!"

"He's up to something," said Rachel.

"But where is he?" Kirsty added.

"I recognise that pink wall," said the queen with a frown. "Oh, if only I could remember!"

At that moment, Jack reached a door in the wall and pushed it open. As he and the goblin went inside, the girls noticed a sign on the door: *Luna's Loom Gallery.*

"Of course!" exclaimed Queen Titania. "He's at Luna the Loom Band Fairy's studio."

Kirsty and Rachel shared a worried look.

"I wonder what he's planning," said Kirsty.

"The studio is just over the brow of that hill," said Queen Titania, pointing to a purple hill behind the palace.

"Girls, will you fly there now and warn
Luna? You can't miss her studio – you'll
recognise the beautiful pink walls."

The girls agreed at once, and a few
seconds later they were zooming through
the bright blue sky towards the brow
of the hill. Below, white flowers dotted
the green grass like stars. As they flew
over the top of the hill, they saw a large
coral-pink building straight ahead of
them. It seemed to glow in the sunlight.

"Look – there's a door," said Rachel, pointing to the front of the building.

They swooped in and saw a beautiful fairy bending over a loom. She was wearing a pale pink cropped jumper and a flowing cream skirt, and her arms were covered in colourful loom-band bracelets. She didn't seem to have heard the girls arriving.

"Hello, are you Luna?" asked Kirsty.

The fairy turned to them with a smile. A fringe plait decorated her brown, wavy hair, and her eyes sparkled with merriment.

"That's me," she said. "Have you come to look around my gallery?"

"No, we're Rachel and Kirsty, and Queen Titania sent us," said Rachel, stumbling over her words as she spoke. "We've come to warn you about Jack Frost!"

No Loom in the Room!

Quickly, the girls told their story. Luna frowned.

"He could be planning to steal my new patterns and designs," she said.

She flew up to a set of drawers on a high wall and opened each one. When she flew back down, she was smiling.

"All my designs are still here," she told the girls. "There's nothing else that Jack Frost could possibly want—"

She broke off and went pale.

"What is it?' asked Rachel in concern.

"I have a special magical object on display in the gallery at the moment," said Luna. "My golden loom is very important, because it makes sure that all loom-band creations turn out well. What if something's happened to it?"

"We saw Jack Frost heading into the

gallery in the Seeing Pool," Kirsty said
in dismay. "He must be planning to steal
the golden loom!"

Luna darted through an archway and
along a corridor, swiftly followed by
Rachel and Kirsty. They swooped into
a large gallery full of loom-band models
and designs, and then Luna let out a cry
of alarm. A pedestal stood
at the centre of the
gallery, but there
was no golden
loom upon it.
Instead, there
was a tiny
golden model
of Jack Frost –
sticking his tongue
out at them!

Luna looked very
upset. "Without
my golden loom,
no one will be
able to use loom
bands properly
here or in the
human world,"
she said. "I have
to find it – but where
could Jack Frost have hidden it?"

"He was at a loom-band workshop
when we saw him," said Rachel. "I
expect he's gone back there with the
loom, to make what he wants."

"Yes," said Luna. "My magical golden
loom will make him the best loom-band
artist in the world, and everyone else will
lose their skills."

34

"Let's go back to the café and look for him," Kirsty said.

Luna waved her wand and a ribbon of fairy dust coiled around the three friends, lifting them off their feet and spinning everyone around. When the dizziness faded, they found themselves standing outside the café once again.

Luna tucked herself under a lock of Kirsty's hair, and the girls walked in and started to work their way around the busy café. But as they searched for Jack Frost, the other children started to complain.

"My loom broke!"

"These loom bands keep snapping!"

Even Oscar was struggling to link his bands together, and one little girl was crying because she couldn't make her bands connect. Sarah was trying  to help everyone, but she was also struggling to use the looms, and looked very upset.

"I can't understand it," the girls heard her say to herself. "I'm all fingers and thumbs."

"I don't think Jack Frost is here," said

Luna in Kirsty's ear. "We should go back to Fairyland."

"Wait!" cried Rachel.

She pointed at a large green foot sticking out from beneath one of the café tables.

"That's a goblin foot!" said Kirsty.

Together, the best friends crouched down and peered underneath the table. Two plump goblins were sitting there, flicking loom bands at each other.

"Stop that!" cried Rachel. "Don't you know that it's dangerous to flick bands at people? Someone could get hurt!"

The goblins turned to her and stuck out their tongues.

"Shut up and leave us alone," said the first goblin.

"Thanks to Jack Frost, we can do anything we like with loom bands," said the second.

"I don't believe you," said Kirsty, thinking quickly. "Jack Frost isn't clever enough to be able to use a loom – we

saw him in here earlier and he couldn't
even make a simple bracelet."

"How dare you?" exclaimed the first
goblin, opening his eyes wide. "Jack
Frost is a loom-band genius!"

"He's got a magical loom and soon
he'll have all the newest loom bands in
the human world," added the second
goblin. "So there!"

"That's impossible," said Rachel.

"There's no way he could collect all the loom bands from all the shops across the world so quickly."

"That shows how much you know, stupid!" shouted the first goblin. "Jack Frost is a million times cleverer than you! He doesn't need to go to all the shops, he can just take them from the biggest loom-band factory in the world!"

As soon as he had spoken, the goblin realised that he had said too much. He clapped his hands over his mouth as if he could stop the words from escaping,

but it was too late. Luna flew out from under Kirsty's hair and hovered in front of him.

"Thank you for the information," she said. "Now I know exactly where to find Jack Frost!"

"Let's get out of here!" said the second goblin with a gulp.

"That goes for us too," said Luna. "We need to get to the largest loom-band factory in the world – right now!"

Following Frost

As the goblins scampered out of the café, the girls crept under the table. There were so many looms and loom bands breaking that no one noticed what they were doing. Luna raised her wand, and in the blink of an eye Rachel and Kirsty were standing in a big factory warehouse, surrounded by huge boxes.

"These boxes are filled with loom bands," said Rachel, reading the labels on the side. "Look – they're going to countries all over the world."

Luna flew across to look at the labels, but just then they heard squawks and cackles coming from another part of the warehouse.

"Come on!" cried Kirsty.

She and Rachel ran towards the sound, with Luna fluttering between them. Ahead, they saw five goblins bending over open boxes. They were stuffing loom bands into large sacks. As each sack was filled, it was passed along a line of goblins towards the window. A rope was dangling down and as the sacks were attached to the rope, they were pulled up out of sight.

44

"They're *stealing!*" gasped Rachel.

"Wait here," said Luna in a low voice. "I'll go and see what's happening to the sacks."

She zoomed out through the window, over the heads of the goblins. Rachel and Kirsty watched as more sacks were hoisted up through the window. A few seconds later, Luna came back looking very upset.

"Jack Frost is sitting on the roof!" she told the girls. "He's pulling the bags up and using his wand to send them somewhere!"

"Then we have to stop him before he empties the warehouse," said Kirsty in a determined voice. "But how?"

Rachel looked around and spotted an emergency alarm on the wall.

"Maybe we should set that off," she said.

"But it's only for emergencies," said Kirsty in a nervous voice.

"This *is* an emergency!" Rachel exclaimed, hurrying towards it.

Taking a deep breath, she picked up the tiny hammer next to the alarm and used it to break the glass. Immediately a loud wailing sound echoed around the warehouse, and the girls heard shouts

and footsteps running their way.

"Luna, could you turn us into fairies?" asked Kirsty. "I don't want to have to explain why we're here!"

Luna waved her wand and the girls immediately shrank to fairy size, while beautiful wings appeared on their backs. They fluttered into the air as the factory workers came running around the corner and spotted  the goblins. At the sound of the alarm the naughty creatures had scattered in a panic, and they were now running into boxes, walls and each other.

"Stop, thieves!" shouted the factory workers, racing towards them.

The goblins squealed and started jumping out of the window. The last one escaped just in the nick of time.

"Come on, let's go up to the roof," said Rachel, feeling brave. "We have to stop Jack Frost before he escapes too."

The three fairies swooped out over the heads of the factory workers, and zoomed up to the roof. Jack Frost was still sitting there, and Kirsty saw that he had the golden loom tucked under his cloak. But to their surprise, he didn't look cross. He was holding a big bag of loom bands and grinning.

"You can't stop me now!" he cackled, heaving the bag onto his shoulder. "I already have enough bands for my first designs, and whenever I want more I'll just come back here!"

There was a crack of blue lightning and he disappeared, but as he vanished a few loom bands showered down from where had been standing. Rachel and Kirsty felt upset, but Luna smiled.

"Don't worry," she said. "His bag had a hole in it, and that means he has left a loom-band trail – which I can follow!"

"Amazing!" exclaimed Kirsty.

Luna took their hands.

"Don't let go," she said. "I have no idea where the trail will take us."

The girls held on tight as a swirling kaleidoscope of colour surrounded them,

49

while loom bands whirled past their
surprised eyes.

"Hold on!" they heard Luna cry.
"We're going back to Fairyland!"

The colours and loom bands whizzed
around them, faster and faster...and then
very suddenly the colours faded and the
spinning stopped. The three friends were
standing in a shabby, damp room with
curved walls.

"I know this room!" Rachel exclaimed.
"We've been here before."

"Yes," Kirsty agreed with a little shiver.
"This is the highest room in one of the
towers of Jack Frost's Ice Castle."

Luna flew to the tiny
arched window and
looked outside.

"You're right," she
said, nodding. "I
can see the forest in
front of the castle,
and the sky is grey
and cloudy. What a
miserable place!"

"If the loom-band trail brought us here,
then your golden loom must be here
too," said Rachel. "We have to search
the castle for it!"

Prisoners in the Tower

Feeling nervous but determined, the three fairies peered out of the door. There was no one in sight, so they fluttered down the winding steps to the next tower room. They could hear voices through the thick oak door.

"Now I have this magical golden loom, I'm going to create the most amazing coat there's ever been," Jack Frost was boasting. "And I'm going to make a grand sculpture of ME, and then a brand-new castle made entirely of loom bands."

The fairies heard goblins clapping and cheering, and then everything went quiet. They flew closer to the door and pressed their ears against it. Then they got a terrible surprise – the door was flung open and they somersaulted though the air into the room.

Poor Luna actually bumped into Jack Frost. With a cry of rage, he snatched at her and managed to grab her wand out of her hand. Rachel and Kirsty darted forward and pulled her out of his way.

"Come back here!" Jack Frost shrieked. "Catch them!"

His goblins hurled themselves after the fairies, who zoomed out of the room and back up the winding stairs. Goblin feet slapped against the cold stone steps as Rachel, Kirsty and Luna flew into the topmost tower room.

"Quickly, out of the window!" Kirsty gasped. "They can't follow us there!"

But a dreadful shock was waiting for them. The window was shut and locked! As they fluttered against the glass, Jack Frost stopped in the doorway of the room, laughing cruelly.

"There's no way out," he said, twirling Luna's wand around his long, bony fingers. "Now you're my prisoners – forever!"

He slammed the door and the fairies heard the key turn in the lock.

"Two goblins stay here and don't move," Jack Frost bellowed. "Now I've finally got some fairy prisoners, you had better not let them escape. Don't even talk to them!"

His footsteps clattered down the stairs.

Tears sparkled in Luna's eyes and she buried her head in her hands.

"This is all my fault," she said in a muffled voice. "I've led you into a trap."

Rachel and Kirsty sat down on either side of her and put their arms around her shoulders. They felt scared too, but they couldn't bear to see her so upset.

"We'll find a way out," said Kirsty.

"Of course we will," said Rachel, making her voice sound as cheerful as possible. "Jack Frost is not as clever as three friends working together!"

"There might even be something in this room that could help us to open the window," said Kirsty, jumping up and looking around.

Luna dried her eyes and stood up too. But after a few minutes of searching, all they had found were three stale Brussels sprouts and a small mouse.

"Nothing," said Luna, her shoulders slumping.

"Wait a minute," said Rachel. "I'm still wearing the loom-band bracelet that Kirsty made for me."

She pulled her bracelet off and handed it to Luna.

"You're a loom-band expert," she said. "Couldn't you use this in some way, even without your wand?"

Luna took the bracelet and gave a little smile.

"This might just work," she said. "Your bracelet was made before the golden loom was stolen, so it's still strong."

She flew over to the window and carefully fed the bracelet through the narrow gap to the catch on the outside.

Rachel and Kirsty watched, hardly
daring to breathe, as Luna's tiny fingers
kept trying to hook the bracelet around
the catch. Twice she failed, but the third
time there was a little click, the bracelet
fell to the ground below and the window
swung open. They were free!

Pausing only to
share a relieved
hug, they flew
out through
the window
and down to
the tower room
below. Luckily, its
windows were open, so
it was easy to slip inside and hide behind
the billowing curtains.

Jack Frost was sitting cross-legged

in the middle of the room, surrounded
by stolen bags of loom bands. He was
using the golden loom and making his
coat with flying fingers. All around him,
goblins were making their own designs,
without looms.

"This is hard," grumbled one of the
goblins. "Why can't we use the loom for
a bit?"

"Because you are not a loom-band
genius like me," snapped Jack Frost
without looking up. "Don't ask stupid
questions."

"There's your wand!" whispered Kirsty,
pointing to where Luna's missing wand
was lying on the floor, forgotten.

"We have to try to get the wand *and*
the loom," said Rachel. "But how, in a
room full of goblins?"

Teamwork!

"I've got an idea!" said Kirsty. "Perhaps
we can force the goblins to leave the
room by making them chase their
designs."

"What do you mean?" asked Rachel.

Kirsty started to unpick the loom-band
bracelet that Rachel had made for her.

"If we flick our loom bands at the things the goblins have made, we should be able to knock them through the door and down the stairs," she explained. "Then the goblins will chase them."

"But it's naughty to flick loom bands," said Rachel, looking uncomfortable.

"We're not flicking them at the goblins, only at what they've made," said Kirsty. "Besides, without Luna's wand, these bracelets are the only things we have to help us."

She shared out the loom bands and then all three of them crouched down and took aim. Being very careful not to hit the goblins, they flicked their bands across the room and sent three loom-band hair bows flying out through the open door. Their owners let out

infuriated yells as their creations bounced
down the winding stairs.

"Now we have to go all the way to
the bottom of the tower to get them,"
grumbled one goblin. "These loom bands
are tricky!"

"Idiots," said Jack Frost. "I bet you
wish you were as skilful as me."

As the first three goblins headed out of the room, the fairies aimed at another three objects.

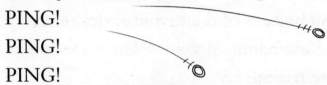

PING!

PING!

PING!

They too went flying out through the door. Each goblin went chasing after his design, until eventually there were no goblins left in the room – only Jack Frost.

"This is our chance!" said Rachel. "Luna, can you lock the door to stop the goblins coming back? I'll grab the wand, and Kirsty, you try to get the loom. We have to do everything at the same time, or else Jack Frost might be fast enough to stop us."

"It's now or never!" Kirsty agreed. "Let's go!"

The three fairies zoomed in through the window, each determined to succeed in her own mission. Luna pushed the door as hard as she could and it shut with a loud bang. As she heaved the bolt home with all her strength, Jack Frost leapt to his feet and yelled out. He hadn't seen Kirsty fluttering behind him, darting left and right as she tried to reach the loom in his hand.

At the same
moment,
Rachel
dived
down
to his
feet and
scooped
up the
wand.

"Luna,
catch!" she yelled,
throwing the wand through the air.

"NO!" cried Jack Frost, lunging
towards her. "Goblins, get in here now!"

Luna caught her wand and Jack Frost
let out another screech of fury. He
clutched at his spiky hair in rage, and the
loom fell from his grasp.

"Got it!" cried Kirsty, swooping between his legs and catching the loom just before it hit the floor.

She zoomed towards Luna while goblins battered on the locked door and Jack Frost lunged after her.

"Hold on to me!" Luna shouted.

Rachel and Kirsty grabbed Luna's shoulders as Jack Frost pulled out his wand. A crackling bolt of blue lightning came straight towards them!

Rachel and Kirsty squeezed their eyes shut and Luna waved her wand.

A split second later the three fairies were back in Luna's gallery, their hearts racing. They had disappeared just before the lightning could hit them.

"Thank you for saving us," said Kirsty, handing the golden loom to Luna.

"Thank *you* for saving my loom," said
Luna, placing it back on the pedestal
where it belonged. "Without you, I
would still be stuck in Jack Frost's tower-
room prison!"

The three fairies hugged happily, and
then Luna took a step back.

"It's time for me to send you back to
where you belong," she said, smiling.
"You've got a loom-band workshop to
finish!"

The girls waved as fairy dust coiled
around them, and a few seconds later
they were back under the table in the
café. They crept out and sat down beside
Oscar again. Everyone seemed peaceful
and relaxed. One girl was making a
beautiful collection of rings, and Oscar
had already made a good start on his

handlebar covers. The girls smiled at each other.

"This is a perfect ending to our adventure," said Rachel, looking around at all the busily weaving children.

"We've helped Luna and we've made sure that the workshop wasn't ruined."

"You're right," said Kirsty. "There's just one thing left for us to do."

"What's that?" asked Rachel, looking a bit puzzled.

Kirsty pushed a loom towards her and started to pick out some rainbow-coloured loom bands.

"Start weaving," she said with a happy grin. "We both need new bracelets!"

Now it's time for Kirsty and Rachel to help...

Heidi the Vet Fairy

Read on for a sneak peek...

Rachel Walker opened her eyes and saw the early-morning sun making shadow patterns on the ceiling. For a moment she couldn't think why she felt so excited. Then she remembered. Today, she and her best friend Kirsty Tate were going to work in a vet's surgery. She sat up and looked across the room. Kirsty was still fast asleep in her bed.

"Wake up, Kirsty!" said Rachel, swinging her legs out of bed. "I can't wait to see all the animals!"

Kirsty sat up and rubbed her eyes. Then she gave a huge smile.

"I was dreaming that we were vets," she said. "Today is going to be so much fun!"

Rachel was staying with Kirsty for half term, but they hadn't expected her visit to be quite so exciting. On the first day of the holiday, Kirsty's next-door neighbour Lisa had popped round to ask them an important favour.

Lisa was a vet, and she had just opened her own surgery in the village. She had arranged for some local journalists to come for an open day, so they could write reviews in their papers. She was hoping that they would say good things in their reports so that people would bring their animals to her.

Lisa had asked Rachel and Kirsty if they would help her out on the open day. They were going to take care of the journalists as they looked around the surgery. The girls would be making cups of tea and coffee, serving sandwiches and other refreshments, and keeping the waiting rooms nice and tidy.

"It was kind of Lisa to have uniforms made in our size," said Rachel as she pulled on the blue tunic with its white logo. "We're really going to look like part of the team."

"I think that being a vet must be one of the best jobs in the world," said Kirsty. "I'd love to spend every day helping poorly animals get well again."

"I hope that the journalists say nice things about Lisa's surgery," said Rachel. "It's very useful to have a good vet nearby."

She stroked Kirsty's pet cat, Pearl, who gave a loud purr.

"Pearl agrees!" said Kirsty with a laugh.

"I hope that we get to spend some time with the animals too," said Rachel. "I wonder what different sorts of pets we'll meet."

"A kangaroo would be fun!" said Kirsty.

"Or a dolphin," said Rachel, with a secret smile at her best friend.

Kirsty smiled back. She guessed that Rachel was remembering the wonderful adventure they had shared with Ally the Dolphin Fairy and her dolphin friend

Echo. Ever since they had first met on Rainspell Island, they had made many fairy friends and had lots of happy adventures together.

Read Heidi the Vet Fairy
to find out what adventures are in store
for Kirsty and Rachel!

Competition!

Win a Loom Band Masterclass!

Loom band expert and YouTube star Jasmine Starler offers you and your best friend a personal lesson on how to make fabulous loom band creations in your very own home!

For your chance to win, send us a photo of your Rainbow Magic-inspired loom band designs. Be as creative as you like!

Send your photos to ad@hachettechildrens.co.uk, with the email subject line "Rainbow Magic Loom Band Competition".

Alternatively, post your photos to:

Rainbow Magic Loom Band Competition,
338 Euston Road, London, NW1 3BH

Entrants must be signed up to the Rainbow Magic newsletter to enter.

Sign up now at www.rainbowmagicbooks.co.uk

Join in the magic online by signing up
to the Rainbow Magic fan club!

Meet the fairies, play games and
get sneak peeks at the latest books!

There's fairy fun for everyone at

www.rainbowmagicbooks.co.uk

You'll find great activities, competitions, stories and
fairy profiles, and also a special newsletter.

Find a fairy with
your name!